# THE EGYPTIAN CINDERELLA

by Shirley Climo • illustrated by Ruth Heller

HarperCollins*Publishers*

THE EGYPTIAN CINDERELLA
Text copyright © 1989 by Shirley Climo
Illustrations copyright © 1989 by Ruth Heller
For information address HarperCollins Children's Books, a division of
HarperCollins Publishers, 10 East 53rd Street, New York, NY 10022.

Library of Congress Cataloging-in-Publication Data
Climo, Shirley.
    The Egyptian Cinderella / by Shirley Climo ; illustrated by Ruth
Heller.
        p.    cm.
    Summary: In this version of Cinderella set in Egypt in the sixth
century B.C., Rhodopis, a slave girl, eventually comes to be chosen
by the Pharaoh to be his queen.
    ISBN 0-690-04822-X.—ISBN 0-690-04824-6 (lib. bdg.)
    ISBN 0-06-443279-3 (pbk.)
    [1. Fairy tales.   2. Folklore—Egypt.]   I. Heller, Ruth, 1924–
ill.   II. Title.
PZ8.C56Eg   1989                                          88-37547
398.2′0932—dc19                                                CIP
[E]                                                             AC

First Harper Trophy edition, 1992.

*For my grandchildren*
S.C.


*To Cinderella's loving master*
R.H.

Long ago, in the land of Egypt, where the green Nile River widens to meet the blue sea, there lived a maiden called Rhodopis. When she was still a small child, Rhodopis had been stolen by pirates. She was snatched from her home in Greece, taken across the sea to Egypt, and there sold as a slave.

Like the Egyptian servant girls, Rhodopis went to the water's edge each day to wash clothes or to gather the reeds that grew along the riverbank. But Rhodopis looked different from the Egyptian girls. Their eyes were brown and hers were green. Their hair hung straight to their shoulders, while the breeze blew hers into tangles. Their skin glowed like copper, but her pale skin burned red beneath the sun. That was how she got her name, for Rhodopis meant "rosy-cheeked" in Greek.

"Rosy Rhodopis!" scoffed the servant girls, hissing her name between their teeth.

Rhodopis pretended not to hear, but she blushed rosier than ever.

Although her master was kind, he was old and liked to doze beneath a fig tree. He seldom heard the servant girls tease Rhodopis. He never saw them ordering her about.

"Hurry, Rhodopis!" they would shout at her. "The geese are in the garden, eating up the onions!"

"Mend my robe!"

"I'm hungry, Rhodopis! Bake the bread!"

Rhodopis always hurried to do their bidding, for the Egyptian girls were household servants and she was only a slave.

Rhodopis found friends among the animals instead. Birds ate crumbs from her hands. She coaxed a monkey to sit upon her shoulder and charmed a hippopotamus with her songs. It would raise its huge head from the muddy water and prick its small ears to listen.

Sometimes, when her chores were done and the day had cooled, Rhodopis would dance for her animal companions. She twirled so lightly that her tiny bare feet scarcely touched the ground. One evening her master awakened to see her dance.

"No goddess is more nimble!" he called out. "Such a gift deserves reward." He tugged his chin whiskers, thinking, and then declared, "You shall go barefoot no longer."

Her master ordered a pair of dainty slippers made especially for Rhodopis. The soles were of real leather, and the toes were gilded with rose-red gold. Now when Rhodopis danced, her feet sparkled like fireflies.

The rose-red slippers set Rhodopis more apart than ever. The Egyptian servant girls were jealous, for they wore clumsy sandals woven from papyrus. Out of spite they found new tasks for her to do, keeping Rhodopis so busy that she was too tired to dance at night.

One evening, Kipa, who was chief among the servant girls, announced, "Tomorrow we sail for Memphis to see the Pharaoh. His Majesty is going to hold court for all his subjects."

"There will be musicians and dancing," said another servant girl, eyeing the rose-red slippers.

"There will be feasting," added a third.

"Poor Rhodopis! You must stay behind," Kipa jeered. "You have linen to wash and grain to grind and the garden to weed."

The next morning, just as Ra the Sun was climbing into the sky, Rhodopis followed the servant girls to the riverbank. Kipa wore a necklace of blue beads. Bracelets jingled on the wrists of the second. The third had tied a many-colored sash about her waist. Although Rhodopis wore a plain tunic, on her feet were the rose-red slippers. Perhaps they will let me come along to see the Pharaoh after all, she thought. But the three servant girls poled their raft around the bend in the river without giving Rhodopis a backward glance.

Rhodopis sighed, and turned to the basket piled high with dirty clothes. "Wash the linen, weed the garden, grind the grain." She slapped the wooden paddle against the cloth in time to her song.

The hippopotamus, tired of so dull a tune, pushed out of the reeds and splashed into the river.

"Shame!" cried Rhodopis, shaking her paddle. "You splattered mud on my beautiful slippers!"

She polished the shoes on the hem of her tunic
until the rosy gold glittered in the sun. Then she
carefully put them on the bank behind her.

"Wash the linen, weed the garden . . ." Rhodopis
began again, when suddenly a shadow fell on the
water. Rhodopis jumped up. A great falcon, the symbol
of the god Horus, circled in the sky with wings spread
so wide that they blotted out the sun.

"Greetings to you, Proud Horus," Rhodopis
murmured. She bowed her head and felt a rush of air
on the back of her neck.

When Rhodopis dared to lift her eyes, she saw the falcon soar away. Dangling from his talons was one of her beautiful slippers. "Stop!" she pleaded. "Come back!"

But the bird did not heed her. He flew toward the sun until he was no more than a dark speck against the gold.

Rhodopis bit her tongue. One shoe was worse than none at all. Now she'd have to dance like a stork, hopping about on one foot, and even the monkey would laugh. Rhodopis tucked the slipper into her tunic and returned to her laundry, salting the river with her tears.

After Rhodopis had lost sight of the falcon, the mighty bird followed the course of the Nile to the city of Memphis, to the square where the Pharaoh was holding court. There the falcon watched and waited.

The Pharaoh's name was Amasis. On his head he wore the red-and-white crown of the Two Egypts. The double crown was heavy and pinched his ears. He preferred driving his chariot fast as the wind to sitting on the throne. Amasis yawned.

At that very moment, the falcon dropped the rose-red slipper into his lap.

The slipper was so bright that Amasis thought it was a scrap of the sun. Then he saw the falcon wheeling overhead.

"The god Horus sends me a sign!" exclaimed the Pharaoh. He picked up the rose-red slipper. "Every maiden in Egypt must try this shoe! She whose foot it fits shall be my queen. That is the will of the gods."

Amasis dismissed the court, called for his chariot, and began his search at once.

When the Egyptian servant girls arrived in Memphis, they found the throne empty and the streets deserted.

They were so angry on their return that even seeing Rhodopis without her rose-red slipper did not please them. "Slaves are better off barefoot," snapped Kipa.

The Pharaoh journeyed to distant cities. He tracked the desert where pyramids tower over the sand, and he climbed the steep cliffs where falcons nest. The rose-red slipper was always in his hand. Wherever he went, women and girls, rich or poor, flocked to try on the slipper. But none could fit into so small a shoe.

The longer Amasis searched, the more determined he became to marry the maiden who had lost the tiny slipper. He summoned his royal barge and vowed to visit every landing along the Nile. The barge was hung with sails of silk. Trumpets blared and oarsmen rowed to the beat of gongs. The din was so dreadful that, when the barge rounded the bend in the river, Rhodopis fled in alarm. But the servant girls ran to the water's edge.

"Now we will see the Pharaoh!" cried Kipa.

Amasis held up the rose-red slipper. "Whoever can wear this shoe shall be my queen."

The servant girls knew that shoe, and knew its owner, too. Yet they clapped their hands over their mouths and said nothing. If one of them could wear it . . .

First Kipa, then the others, tried to put on the slipper. Each cramped her foot and curled her toes and squeezed until tears ran down her cheeks. Still her heel hung over.

"Enough!" said Amasis wearily. He would have set sail again had he not chanced to see Rhodopis peering through the rushes.

"Come!" he commanded. "You must try this rose-red slipper."

The servant girls gawked openmouthed as the Pharaoh kneeled before Rhodopis. He slipped the tiny shoe on her foot with ease. Then Rhodopis pulled its mate from the folds of her tunic.

"Behold!" cried Amasis. "In all this land there is none so fit to be queen!"

"But Rhodopis is a slave!" protested one of the servant girls.

Kipa sniffed. "She is not even Egyptian."

"She is the most Egyptian of all," the Pharaoh declared. "For her eyes are as green as the Nile, her hair as feathery as papyrus, and her skin the pink of a lotus flower."

The Pharaoh led Rhodopis to the royal barge, and with every step, her rose-red slippers winked and sparkled in the sun.

# Author's Note

The tale of Rhodopis (ra-*doh*-pes) and the rose-red slippers is one of the world's oldest Cinderella stories. It was first recorded by the Roman historian Strabo in the first century B.C.

The story is both fact and fable. Rhodopis is believed to have been born in northern Greece, kidnapped by pirates as a child, and sold to a rich man on the island of Samos. One of her fellow slaves was a homely little man named Aesop, who told her wonderful fables about animals.

When Rhodopis was almost grown, she was taken to Egypt and bought by a man named Charaxos. Her new master was also Greek, and he gave many gifts and favors to Rhodopis. In those days, a fortunate slave might live far better than a hired servant. The servants, although free, were poor and lived in mud huts, while a chosen slave enjoyed the comforts of the master's villa.

The existence of the rose-red slippers is possible. Ancient Egyptian gold was sometimes mixed with iron, which gave it a reddish hue. In retelling this story, I preferred to have the gilded slippers stolen by a falcon, although some references name the bird as an eagle. Horus, Egyptian sky god and deity of the living pharaohs, was believed to appear on earth as a falcon.

What *is* fact is that a Greek slave girl, Rhodopis, married the Pharaoh Amasis (ah-*may*-ses) (Dynasty XXVI, 570–526 B.C.) and became his queen.